How to use this book

There are important activities which will help prepare your child for reading the story. When he or she has read the story, there are further activities which will help reinforce what has been learnt.

☆ Have fun talking about the pictures.

☆ Encourage your child to read the engaging story again and again for fun and practice.

☆ Use the Star checklist on page 3 to build your child's confidence as he or she colours in a star after each activity.

Six steps for reading success

1 Practise reading the Speed sounds before the story.
2 Read the Green and Red words before the story.
3 Read the story.
4 Re-read the story to reinforce meaning.
5 Answer the questions about the story.
6 Practise reading the Speed words.

Give your child lots of praise and encouragement. Have fun!

In the bath

I can read the Speed sounds.

I can read the Green words.

I can read the Red words.

I can read the story.

I can answer the questions about the story.

I can read the Speed words.

Say the Speed sounds

Consonants

*Ask your child to say the sounds (not the letter names)
clearly and quickly, in and out of order. Make sure
he or she does not add 'uh' to the end of the sounds,
e.g. 'f' not 'fuh'.*

f	l	m	n	r	s ss	v	z	sh	th	ng nk

b	c k ck	d	g	h	j	p	qu	t	w	x	y	ch

Each box contains one sound.

Vowels

*Ask your child to say each vowel sound and then the word,
e.g. 'a', 'at'.*

at	hen	in	on	up	day	see	high	blow	zoo

Read the Green words

*For each word ask your child to read the separate sounds, e.g. 'p-u-t',
'd-u-ck' and then blend the sounds together to make the word, e.g. 'put',
'duck'. Sometimes one sound is represented by more than one letter, e.g. 'ck',
'th', 'sh'. These are underlined.*

put   duck   got   in   his   this   wet

ship   big   jug   vest   pants   milk

drink   get   mess

Read the Red words

*Red words don't sound like they look. Read the words out to your child.
Explain that he or she will have to stop and think about how to say the
red words in the story.*

the   said   are   your   was   he

In the bath

Introduction
In this story Ben continues playing when his mum calls him for a bath. When Ben does have his bath, he upsets Mum again ...

"Get in the bath, Ben," said Mum.

"Yes, Mum," said Ben.

"Ben! Get in the bath!"
said Mum.

Ben got in the bath.

Ben was fed up.

Ben got Danny the duck
and put it in the bath.

Splish splish

Ben got his ship and put it in the bath.

Splash splash

Then he got Mum's
big jug.

Splosh splosh

"Stop it, Ben," said Mum. "Your vest and pants are wet!"

"Ben!" said Mum.
"The mat is wet!"

"It is a big wet mess!" said Mum.

"Danny the duck did it," said Ben.

"Then Danny the duck can drink this milk," said Mum. "Bed, Ben!"

Questions to talk about

Ask your child:

Page 8:   Why does Mum have to say "Get in the bath!" twice?

Page 11:   What did Ben put in the bath?

Page 15:   What else did Ben put in the bath?

Page 18:   Why is Mum cross?

Page 20:   Why did Ben say "Danny the duck did it?"
           Do you think Mum is really cross?
           Why do you think this is?

Speed words

Ask your child to read the words across the rows, down the columns and in and out of order, clearly and quickly.

put	duck	the	got	in
his	wet	this	are	was
ship	big	jug	mess	vest
pants	said	your	milk	drink

Help your child to read with phonics

Series created by
Ruth Miskin
Based on an original story
by Gill Munton
Illustrated by
Tim Archbold

Published by
Oxford University Press
Great Clarendon Street
Oxford OX2 6DP

ISBN 9 78019 2757838

10 9 8 7 6 5 4 3 2 1

Printed in China by Imago